How to talk to Tigers

Written By Jacob Tilley

Illustrated by Ruby Thompson

Published by New Generation Publishing in 2012

Copyright © Jacob Tilley 2012

First Edition

The author asserts the moral right under the Copyright, Designs and Patents Act 1988 to be identified as the author of this work.

www.newgeneration-publishing.com

Acknowledgements

Great big thanks to my wonderful illustrator Ruby.

Faye for all your help.

Sophie for your scanning expertise.

Joe Till, Bev, Betty and Rand for the family love.

And for being there to listen to my growlings; Roo,

Lloydie May, Crim, Al Salsa, Kazinki, D's Tommy &
Schwanny.

You can all talk to tigers.

Tigers make the greatest pet's, they just cannot be beaten,

But if you don't look after them, then you could wind up eaten.

So learn some lessons, take some notes, on how to treat your cat,

Learn when to whisper, when to shout and when to nicely chat.

Chapter One; Lazy Tigers

If your tiger's being lazy and won't get out your bed,

And you walk in and shout at him, he'll just bite off
your head.

You must wake him nice and slow; make sure he
doesn't jump,

Because if he does your little head could have a great,
big lump.

So when you talk to lazy tigers, you must remember
this,

Start off in a mellow tone and finish with a hiss.

"Out of bed you lazy tiger, now it's time to rise,

Keep your tail between your legs, no pouncing, no surprise."

Chapter Two; Hungry Tigers

When your tiger's hungry, you must be very wary,

If you forget the rules of speech things can get awfully scary.

His teeth are sharp, his eyes are wide, his belly makes a rumble,

Please don't turn your back on him and make sure not to stumble.

So when talking to a hungry tiger you must tread the line,

Don't be too loud, don't be too quiet and make sure not to whine.

"Come now, come now hungry tiger, now it's time for tea,

I've got you some chicken legs so keep your eyes off me."

Chapter Three; Happy Tigers

If your tiger's happy, then you've got a choice,

You can whisper quietly or use your loudest voice.

Happy Tigers like to play and mess about with friends,

Just don't take him to a farm and let him see those big, fat hens!

Heap your cat with joyous praise whilst ruffling his fur,

Tell him that he's beautiful and listen to him purr.

"Let's go play you happy tiger, take me for a ride,

I'll jump on your stripy back then let's go down the slide."

Chapter Four; Poorly Tigers

If your tiger's poorly, there is something you must do,

Put on a pair of marigolds and rifle through his…

Tigers don't like being poorly, just as much as kids,

And they can't open medicine, paws can't undo the lids.

To find out what is wrong with him you must be very daring,

Get up close and cuddle him and speak so very caring.

"There, there now you poorly tiger, rest your sleepy head,

Have a spoon of medicine and then it's time for bed."

Chapter Five; Excited Tigers

Excited tigers can be pretty tricky to control,

They bound around and knock things down, they jump
and pounce and roll.

They fly through windows, swing from doorframes,
knock over your chair,

If you can't calm him down real quick, you'll be pulling
out your hair!

So do your best to use your voice to keep your tiger
mellow,

Speak nice and calm and nonchalant and definitely
don't bellow!

"Calm right down excited tiger, before you hurt yourself,

All this silly messing round is not good for my health."

Chapter Six; Upset Tigers

When your tiger gets upset you must be understanding,

But if he opens up his mouth, please don't put your hand in!

Tigers sometimes get upset by lots of different things,

Like smelly bottoms, sticky feet, or when your mother sings.

So talk to him in soothing tones and tell him to relax,

Give your cat a great big hug and rub his stripy back.

"Have a hug you upset tiger, blow your snotty snout,

You'll feel better in a while, of that there is no doubt."

Chapter Seven; Naughty Tigers

When your tiger's being naughty, you must be very stern,

Because if you neglect to tell him off, then he'll never learn.

He'll steal your pillow, eat your biscuits, even bite your hand,

You need to let him know, just who's in command.

So stand up tall and raise your voice, shout that tiger down,

Use your deepest scary tone and make sure to wear a frown.

"Don't do that you naughty tiger, that's really not amusing!

You better do just as you're told, it isn't that confusing!"

Chapter Eight; Angry Tigers

If you've got an angry tiger then you must beware,

Grab a cushion, grab a broom and hide behind a chair.

He's growling and he's snarling, there's fire in his eyes,

Starting to approach him really, truly isn't wise.

As for rules of speaking, well, there's not much to be done,

If your tiger's angry then just shut your mouth and run!

"See you later angry tiger; I'll be leaving now,

I'll come back home in a while, I'll see you later! Ciao!"

So there we go now, yes, you've done it, you have passed the test,

You know how to talk to tigers and I'm sure you'll do your best.

Tigers are the greatest pets; they really can't be beaten,

And you know how to talk to them, so now you won't get eaten.